Little Hector

and the Big Idea

Ruth Paul

PUFFIN

Little Hector was a small and playful dolphin.

His favourite game was playing tag
with his Bottlenose cousins.

They **raced** and **chased**, **ducked** and **dived**,
until one day
his big grey cousin called
"Stop!"
and pointed to the horizon.

"Fishing nets," she said,
and everyone turned around.

Hector's second-favourite game was playing ball with Seal and Stingray.

They **tossed** and **turned**, **dipped** and **dunked** ...

until suddenly, their ball unravelled into a mess of floating bags.

"We can't play with those," grumbled Seal,
"they're dangerous."

Hector played his third-favourite game, hide-and-seek, with Octopus.

He shut his eyes and counted to ten.

"Coming, ready or not..."

But Octopus was **far** too easy to find.

So Hector had no choice but to make his own fun.

"Look, I'm a Bottlenose!" he called,
but his cousins were not impressed.

"Get that thing off your nose," said his mother.
"It's not safe – just ask Seagull and Turtle."

"Everything fun is unsafe,"
grumbled Hector.

But, as usual, his mother was right.

Seagull had once suffered a terrible tummy ache
when she swallowed a bottle lid,
and Turtle struggled to swim with his plastic bracelet.

"If only I could do something to make our cove safe," said Hector,
but the problems seemed very, very big
and he was a very small dolphin.

"A small dolphin can still have
big ideas," said his father.

Hector thought and thought.
Fishing nets were dangerous.
Plastic rubbish was dangerous.

Then, suddenly, he had an idea.
Could he use one problem to solve the other?
He leapt out of the water in excitement.

All the creatures of the cove gathered
around Little Hector.

And after hearing his plan,
each of them bravely offered to help.

Seal scoped out the route.

The Bottlenose dolphins checked the currents.

Stingray surveyed the extent of the rubbish,

and Octopus practised his slinky escape moves.

At last it was time for action.
The Bottlenose dolphins swam
round and round to create a current.

Stingray and Seal pushed rubbish into its whirl.

Schools of fish herded the trash into the nets,
and Octopus knotted them together.

fish!

fish!

When the Seagulls cried **"Fish! Fish!"** and circled overhead, the fishermen leapt to their feet and dragged in the nets.

"**Oi!**"
and
"**Holy mackerel!**"

cried the fishermen,
hauling in the biggest pile of rubbish they'd ever seen.

They couldn't even undo the knots
to return the rubbish to the sea.

As they cursed and grumbled
and scratched their heads,
the captain could have sworn
she saw a wonky old turtle waving.

After that day, the fishing boats stayed away.
Rubbish was still a problem, but the creatures of the
cove worked together to keep it away from their home.
Sometimes even the humans helped them out.

And Little Hector?

Hector discovered that
with a little help from his friends,
a very small dolphin could solve
even the biggest of problems.

"Coming,
ready
or not..."